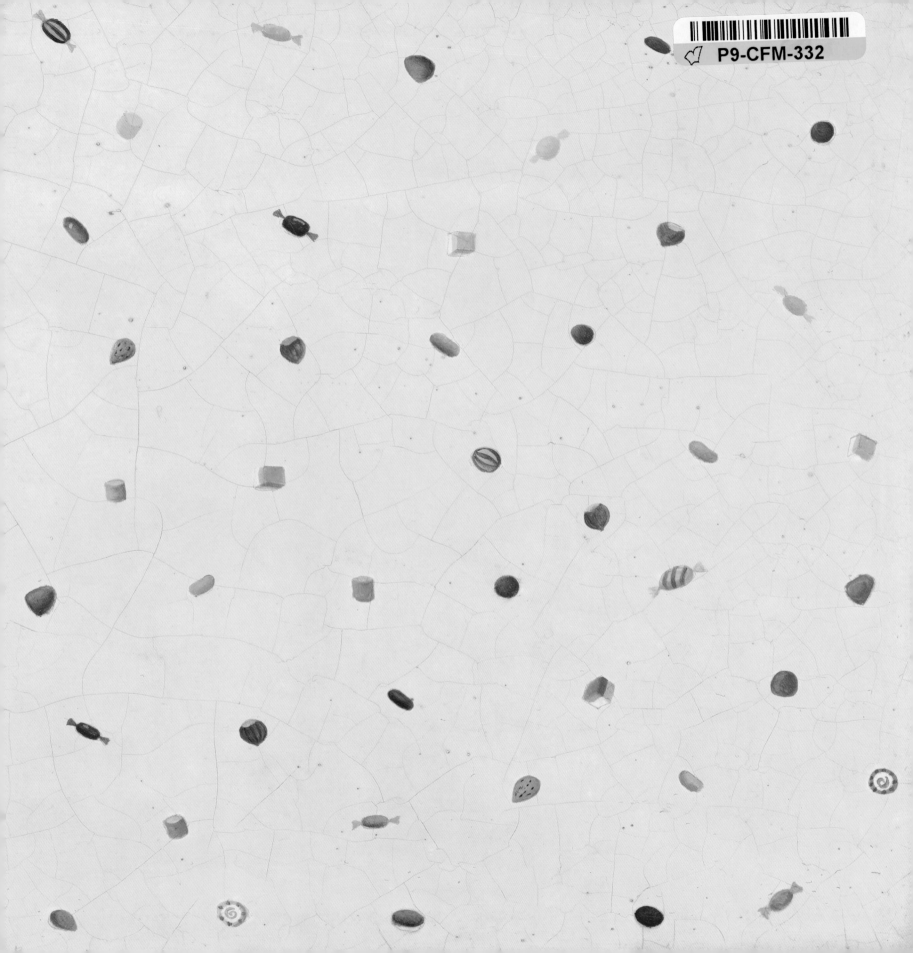

The Nutcracker

illustrations by Alison Jay

Dial Books for Young Readers

an imprint of Penguin Group (USA) Inc.

For Eleanor Esmae—

happy First Birthday. Love from Alison x

DIAL BOOKS FOR YOUNG READERS
A division of Penguin Young Readers Group
Published by The Penguin Group
Penguin Group (USA) Inc., 375 Hudson Street, New York, NY 10014, U.S.A.
Penguin Group (Canada), 90 Eglinton Avenue East, Suite 700, Toronto, Ontario, Canada M4P 2Y3 (a division of Pearson Penguin Canada Inc.)
Penguin Books Ltd, 80 Strand, London WC2R 0RL, England
Penguin Ireland, 25 St. Stephen's Green, Dublin 2, Ireland (a division of Penguin Books Ltd)
Penguin Group (Australia), 250 Camberwell Road, Camberwell, Victoria 3124, Australia (a division of Pearson Australia Group Pty Ltd)
Penguin Books India Pvt Ltd, 11 Community Centre, Panchsheel Park, New Delhi – 110 017, India
Penguin Group (NZ), 67 Apollo Drive, Rosedale, North Shore 0632, New Zealand (a division of Pearson New Zealand Ltd)
Penguin Books (South Africa) (Pty) Ltd, 24 Sturdee Avenue, Rosebank, Johannesburg 2196, South Africa
Penguin Books Ltd, Registered Offices: 80 Strand, London WC2R 0RL, England

Based on the story by E. T. A. Hoffman
Retold by AnnMarie Anderson

Text copyright © 2010 by Penguin Group (USA) Inc.
Illustrations copyright © 2010 by Alison Jay
The publisher does not have any control over and does not assume any
responsibility for author or third-party websites or their content.
Designed by Lily Malcom
Text set in Bromwich
Manufactured in China on acid-free paper

1 3 5 7 9 10 8 6 4 2

Library of Congress Cataloging-in-Publication Data

Jay, Alison.
The Nutcracker / pictures by Alison Jay.
p. cm.
"Based on the story by E.T.A. Hoffman, retold by AnnMarie Anderson"—Copyright p.
Summary: After rescuing her Christmas nutcracker from an army of angry toys, Clara is rewarded by the nutcracker, now a prince,
with a fantastic nighttime journey to a realm of dancing fairies, beautiful palaces, and wonderful things to eat.
ISBN 978-0-8037-3285-8 (hardcover)
[1. Fairy tales. 2. Ballets—Stories, plots, etc. 3. Christmas—Fiction.] I. Anderson, AnnMarie. II. Hoffmann, E. T. A. (Ernst Theodor
Amadeus), 1776–1822. Nussknacker und Mausekönig. III. Nutcracker (Choreographic work) IV. Title.
PZ8.J30Nu 2010
[E]—dc22
2009051657

The art was created using alkyd oil paint on paper with crackling varnish.

It was Christmas Eve and snow fell softly on the ground. Inside, it was warm and cozy, the air filled with the smell of gingerbread. Clara could hardly wait for Godfather Drosselmeyer to arrive for the party.

As if on cue, the door burst open. A poof of snow settled on the stoop. There was Godfather Drosselmeyer, with his flowing cape and curly mustache. "Merry Christmas!" he bellowed, and scooped Clara up in a great big hug.

Godfather Drosselmeyer was a famous toy and clock maker. He could make a toy out of anything, even an empty spool of thread or an old bottle cap. Now the children gathered around as he reached under his cape and produced one bright package after another.

"Thank you!" cried the
children as they tore open
their gifts. Clara's brother Fritz got a
wooden toy sword. Anne got a lovely
doll with sparkling fairy wings. And Ben got a
wind-up mouse that was so fuzzy and gray it
almost looked real.

But Clara knew her present was the best of all. It was a toy
soldier—but not just any toy soldier. If you put a nut between its
teeth and pulled the lever in its back, it cracked the shell right open.

"Oh, thank you," breathed Clara. "I love it!"

Clara passed the Nutcracker around for everyone to try. But Fritz grabbed it and shoved a walnut between its teeth. He pulled the lever down hard—*Snap!* The shell cracked in two, and so did the Nutcracker's jaw.

SNAP!

"Fritz!" Clara cried. "You've broken it!" She cradled the injured toy in her arms.

With a flourish, Godfather Drosselmeyer stepped in. He pulled out a handkerchief and tied it around the Nutcracker's head. "That should do for now," he said. "Tomorrow, I'll get my tools and I'll fix him properly. But now, Mother says it's time for bed."

After saying good night to the party guests, Clara gave the Nutcracker a kiss and placed him gently under the Christmas tree with all of the other toys. Then, reluctantly, she went upstairs to bed.

But try as she might, Clara couldn't sleep. Late that night, she tiptoed back downstairs and curled up beneath the tree, with the Nutcracker snug in her arms. Finally, she drifted off.

Clara woke with a start. The grandfather clock chimed loudly. She glanced around and rubbed her eyes. Something incredible was happening. The Christmas tree appeared to be growing. Larger and larger it rose—right before her eyes!

As the tree grew, so did the toys beneath it. Soon, Clara was standing face-to-face with the Nutcracker.

And then something even stranger happened. An army of mice marched from behind the sofa, led by a very large, very fuzzy gray mouse. Atop his head sat a golden crown. Clara stared. Then shook herself—the mice were headed straight for her!

Suddenly the Nutcracker moved. He pulled a wooden sword from his side and marched forward, shielding Clara from the mice, and leading the toys into battle!

Clara gasped as the Nutcracker and the Mouse King dueled. But the Nutcracker's

wooden sword was no match for the Mouse King's shiny metal one. Clara had to do something. She looked around. There was no time! She tore her slipper from her foot and threw it at the Mouse King with all her might.

The Mouse King crumpled to the ground, his
crown spinning to rest beside him.
Clara couldn't believe her eyes. For as the Mouse
King fell, the Nutcracker magically transformed
into a Prince.

Now he swept the Mouse King's crown from the floor and placed it atop Clara's head. "Thank you," he said. "I've been trapped in the shape of the Nutcracker for many years. But your bravery has broken the Mouse King's spell. Now I am free."

Clara didn't know what to say. She reached up and touched the gold crown on her head, then looked down to see that her nightdress had turned into a magnificent gown.

The Prince held out his hand. "Would you come with me to my kingdom, the
Land of Sweets?" he asked.

"Oh, how lovely!" Clara said as she took the Prince's hand. Together, they stepped
out into the snowy night, where a horse-drawn sleigh waited.

As the sleigh pulled them through the Land of Snow, the stars sparkled like diamonds in the sky. Dazzling snowflakes danced all around them.

Before long, the carriage pulled up to a marvelous castle built with cubes of sugar instead of bricks. The gates surrounding it appeared to be made of . . . peppermint sticks? Clara blinked in disbelief.

"This is where I live—the Marzipan Palace," said the Prince. A beautiful girl had appeared beside him. "And this is the Sugar Plum Fairy."

"You've been missed, dear Prince. Welcome home," said the Sugar Plum Fairy. Then she turned to Clara and smiled warmly. "Welcome to the Land of Sweets," she said.

The Prince explained how Clara had saved his life by bravely defeating the Mouse King. Now the Sugar Plum Fairy took Clara's hands in her own. "We must have a feast!" she declared. "A great banquet in your honor, with delicious food and wonderful dancers!"

Clara and the Prince had barely sat down
when the festivities began. First, waiters
wheeled out an enormous box of chocolates—

but when the lid was removed, two Spanish dancers leaped out, clicking their castanets.

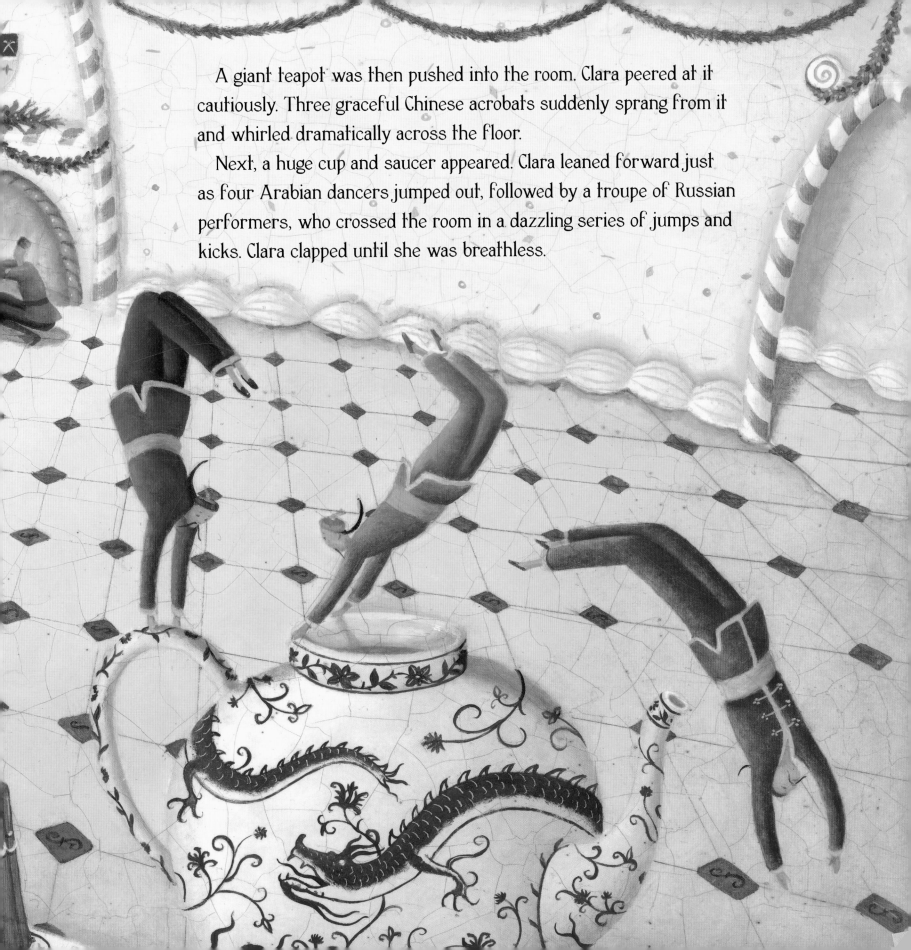

A giant teapot was then pushed into the room. Clara peered at it cautiously. Three graceful Chinese acrobats suddenly sprang from it and whirled dramatically across the floor.

Next, a huge cup and saucer appeared. Clara leaned forward just as four Arabian dancers jumped out, followed by a troupe of Russian performers, who crossed the room in a dazzling series of jumps and kicks. Clara clapped until she was breathless.

After a short pause, Mother Ginger emerged. She wore an enormous skirt—and Clara giggled in surprise as six French children scampered out from beneath it!

Clara drew in her breath, amazed, as the children spun like candy-colored tops around the room.

Finally, a dozen girls wearing brightly colored rose-petal skirts performed an enchanting waltz. As the dance ended, the Sugar Plum Fairy came forward. The Prince joined her, and the two danced a magnificent duet.

Each time the Sugar Plum Fairy spun around,
her sparkling skirt and wings cast the moonlight
in prisms around the room.

As the festivities wound down, Clara stifled a yawn.

"It is time we took you home," the Prince told her softly.

"I don't want to leave just yet," Clara said sleepily.

But as she spoke, her eyes began to close. The Prince picked her up and carried her out to the waiting sleigh. He placed her gently inside and whispered something in the horse's ear. In an instant, the sleigh was whisking Clara home through the snow.

On Christmas morning, Clara woke in her own warm, cozy bed. Her beautiful gown had turned back into a nightdress, and when she reached up for her crown, there was nothing there.

Then Clara noticed a flash of red beside her. It was her Nutcracker—without the handkerchief bandage and perfectly whole!

Clara scooped him up and hugged him close. Though she never told a soul about her adventure, she hoped in her heart that every Christmas Eve might be as magical as this one.

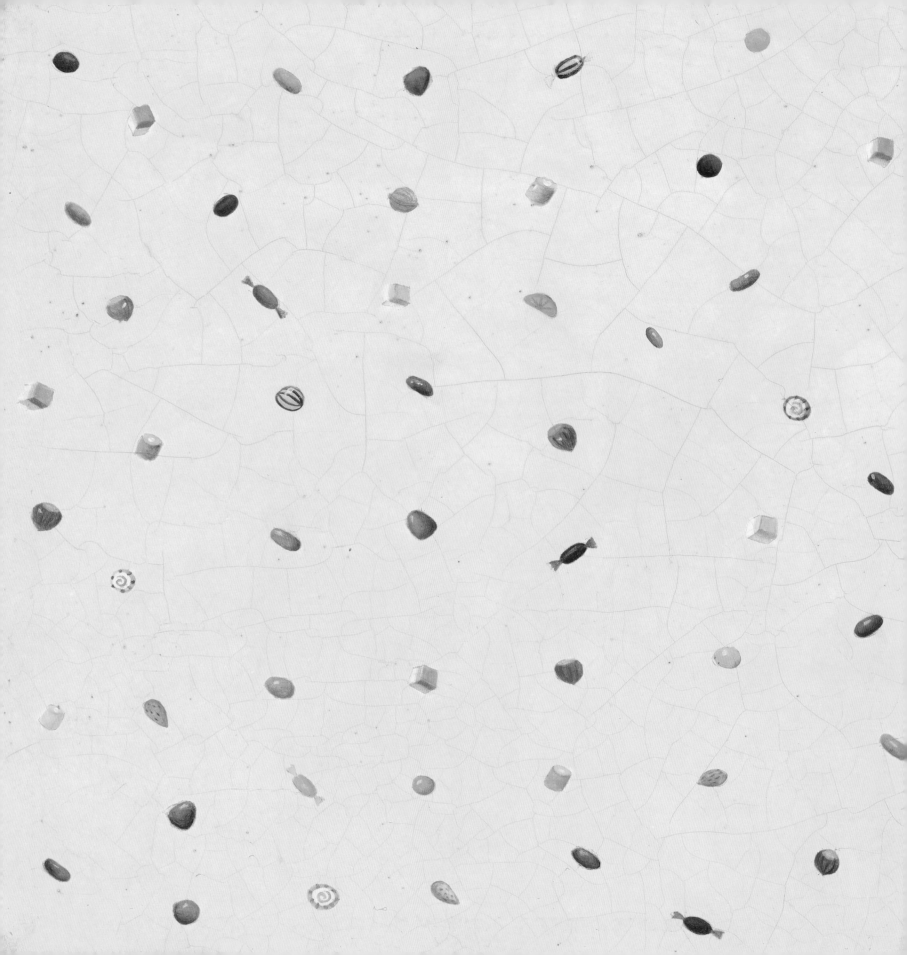